The
Curious Little Kitten

The Curious Little Kitten

By LINDA HAYWARD

Illustrated by MAGGIE SWANSON

GOLDEN PRESS • NEW YORK
Western Publishing Company, Inc., Racine, Wisconsin

nce upon a time there was
a curious little kitten. She lived
in a nice sunny yard behind a nice cozy
house. The little kitten's yard was
surrounded by fences. There was a high
wooden fence on one side, a low
wooden fence on the other side, and in
the back was a red brick wall.

At first the curious little kitten was only curious about the things that were *inside* her yard. She was curious about the flowers and the birds and the garden hose.

She was curious about the clothesline and the
wheelbarrow and the rose bushes. Sometimes it was fun
being so curious, and sometimes it was very uncomfortable.

By and by the little kitten became curious about the things that were *outside* her yard. She began to wonder what was on the other side of those three fences.

One day she peeked through a hole in the high wooden fence. She could see another yard—just like hers—but in that yard there was a small house.

The curious little kitten just had to find out what was inside that small house.

In no time at all, she wriggled through the hole, scurried across the grass, and went right up to the doorway.

She looked into the house. Something brown and furry
was sleeping inside. What could it be? The curious
little kitten crept closer and closer until...

WOOF! WOOF! The brown furry thing woke up. *Ooooh*, was it big! *Ohhhh*, was it loud! The little kitten could not get out of that yard fast enough.

She ran back to her own yard and hid behind the
wheelbarrow. She was very frightened and very certain
that she would never, *never* be curious again.

But the very next day the little kitten found a hole
in the low wooden fence. She looked through it. She
could see another yard—just like hers.

But in that yard there was a small round pond.
The curious little kitten just had to find out what was
in that pond.

In no time at all, the little kitten wriggled through
the hole, scampered across the grass, and went right up
to the edge of the pond.

She peered in. Something bright orange and wiggly was down there, under the water. What could it be? The curious little kitten leaned over farther and farther, closer and closer, until . . .

SPLASH! She tumbled in. *Oooooh*, was it cold! *Ohhhhh*, was it wet! She could not get out of that pond fast enough. She could not get out of that *yard* fast enough!

The little kitten went back to her own yard and found a sunny, dry place to rest. Here in her own yard was where she would stay! Here it was safe!

Being curious could only get a kitten into trouble. She would never, *never* be curious again.

But, the very next day, when she was looking for something to do, the little kitten hopped up to the top of the red brick wall. She only wanted to have a peek.

And there was still
another yard—just like hers.

What was in *that* yard? She had to find out. In no time
at all, the curious little kitten hopped off the wall and
landed right in front of...

Another little kitten! *Ooooooh*, was she surprised! *Ohhhhhh*, was she happy! The curious little kitten could not make friends with that *new* little kitten fast enough.

Sometimes being curious was all right. Sometimes being curious helped a little kitten to find a nice new friend.